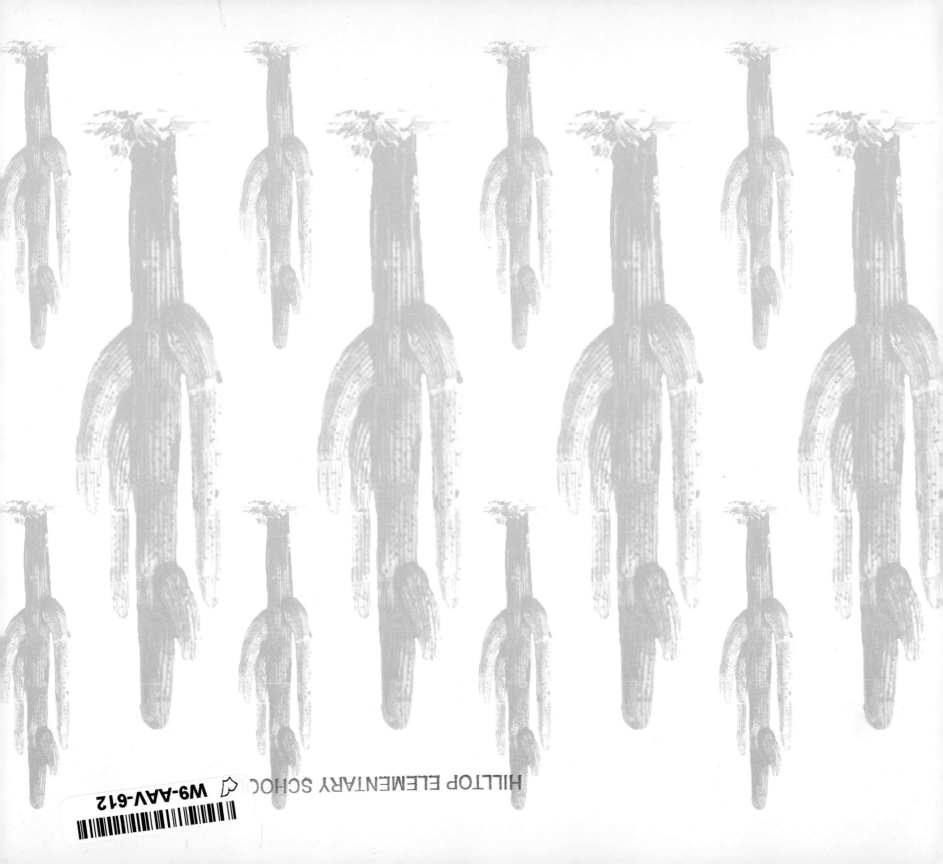

SING DOWN THE RAIN

BY JUDI MOREILLON

ILLUSTRATED BY MICHAEL CHIAGO

KIVA
PUBLISHING, INC.

Text copyright © 1997 by Judith Lynn Moreillon
Illustrations copyright © 1996 by Michael Chiago

Library of Congress Catalog Card Number 97- 070357

Publisher's Cataloging in Publication
(Prepared by Quality Books Inc.)

Moreillon, Judi.
    Sing down the rain / Judi Moreillon; illustrated by Michael Chiago.
    p.cm.
 SUMMARY: A poem about the Tohono O'odham Saguaro Wine Ceremony,
    their most important harvest celebration.
    ISBN: 1-885772-07-6

    1. Tohono O'odham Indians—Rites and ceremonies—Juvenile poetry.
    2. Indians of North America—Arizona—juvenile poetry.
    I. Chiago, Michael. II. Title.

PZ8.3.O7745S564 1997   811'.54   QBI97-40215

Cover design by Steve Marsh
Text design by Jean Lamunière
Printed in Hong Kong

9 8 7 6 5 4

10-04/15M/2004

Kiva Publishing, Walnut, CA

To Trinidad Juan and Maurice Corella
and all the children of the Tohono O'odham nation.

J. M.

To my mother, who gave me all the wisdom and
knowledge of my tradition.

M. C.

Introduction

WE TOHONO O'ODHAM, or Desert People, and our ancestors have lived in the Sonoran Desert for thousands of years. For centuries, we practiced floodwater farming that depended on the summer rains to fill the washes or dry creek beds and water the crops. In addition to this farming method, traditional Desert People were also gatherers, hunters, and traders who proved their resourcefulness living in this harsh climate.

For us, the Desert People, the most important ceremonies are those that bring rain. Late June, when the summer rains are due, marks the beginning of our year. An essential part of the rain-making ceremony is the making and drinking of saguaro fruit wine. Many Desert People live and work in Tucson and on the nearby Tohono O'odham reservations. Each August, a few villages still practice this special ceremony.

We gather the fruits from the saguaro using a long pole to knock the fruits from the tops of these tall cacti. We cook the fruits over an open fire. Then we strain the juice through a grass basket and pour the syrup into jars.

The elders of the village guard the mixture of water and cactus syrup for two days. For two nights, men, women, and children dance in a large circle outside the "Rain House." The chief singers sing and provide music with gourd rattles, and the medicine man walks within the circle holding eagle feathers to catch the wind. The wind will bring the clouds, and the clouds bring the rain.

When the wine is ready, the crier calls the people to come together. The men and women sit in a circle, drink the wine, and recite orations that tell how the wine makes the clouds and the rain.

I work at Indian Oasis Primary School, where I teach O'odham language and culture. As all teachers know, some children take us into their lives. As special friends, we sometimes get invited to birthday parties and other family celebrations. For me, most of these children are of the Tohono O'odham Nation, so the celebrations are in village settings.

Many small O'odham children dance with a traditional dance group. When these children become teenagers, they seem to fade away as they meet new friends, go away to another school, and change so much that I don't recognize them anymore. Once in a while, someone will approach me and call my name. I feel stupid, but I have to ask, "What's your name?"

There are a few young people who dance into their teen years. I see them once in a while as they perform at a gathering on the reservation or at an event in the city. I smile as they perform our tribal dances, happy to see them express their values as they sing and dance in unison.

The words in the following poem remind us of certain young people who are very special. The poem tells us of young men and women who sing and dance for the clouds and the rain. I feel contented because I see our future leaders dancing in front of me. I am not worried about our tribal culture dying out because these dancers are the carriers of tradition.

Children come and go in our lives. The students that have touched us the most are those we have known personally. This book is dedicated to these special people.

DANNY LOPEZ
Big Fields Village
Tohono O'odham Nation of Arizona
May, 1997

A dusty land bakes. Its washes run dry.
The blazing hot sun hovers high in the sky.
Cicadas make music, a sharp scraping sound.
The spreading mesquite trees hang close to the ground.

This spiny land's home to rattlers and quails
And shy little rabbits with soft cotton tails,
Coyotes who howl and sing to the moon,
And mourning doves cooing their sorrowful tune.

Tortoises plod with their homes on their backs,
And the sand records time with animal tracks.
When the sun is white hot, in May and in June,
This dry land is waiting—rain will come soon.

In this desert land live the People who know
How to sing down the rain that makes the crops grow.
A sacred tradition, the elders explain
How wind brings the clouds and clouds bring the rain.

Life-giving clouds, overflowing with light,
Will wait for the wind to send them in flight.
They swell up with rain that's waiting to fall,
To bring cooling water for one and for all.

Tall cactus with arms curving graceful and thin
Will reach out for water when cool rains begin.
With roots that are shallow and spread all around,
They will soak up the rain washing over hard ground.

The life-giving clouds, full of moisture and light,
Form over far mountains, still out of sight.
Clouds swollen with rain that's waiting to fall
Will bring cooling water for one and for all.

Saguaro's white flowers will bloom by starlight.
Reflecting the moon, they will brighten the night.
These blooms become fruits, sweet, juicy and red.
Their juice brings rain magic, the old stories said.

Tall cactus with arms bending and thin
Will swell up with water when sweet rains begin.
With roots that are shallow and spread all around,
They will soak up the rain washing over hard ground.

The life-giving clouds, reflecting sunlight,
Float over far mountains, still out of sight.
Clouds swollen with rain that's waiting to fall
Will bring cooling water for one and for all.

In morning's soft light, the women arrive
To pick the ripe fruits we will need to survive.
In baskets of willow, woven so fine,
They carry the fruits that will make sacred wine.

Saguaro's white flowers, brilliant and bright,
Reflecting the moon, are like stars in the night.
These blooms become fruits, sweet, juicy and red.
Their juice brings rain magic, our grandparents said.

Tall cactus with arms reaching out long and thin
Will fatten with water when cloudbursts begin.
With roots that are shallow and spread all around,
They will soak up the rain washing over hard ground.

The life-giving clouds, so massive and white,
Drift over far mountains, still out of sight.
Clouds swollen with rain that's waiting to fall
Will bring cooling water for one and for all.

Grandfather's fire burns hot like the sun
And cooks the ripe fruit till the syrup is done.
Grandmother's basket is woven just so
To capture the seeds and let syrup flow.

In soft morning light, the women arrive
To harvest the fruits we will need to survive.
In baskets of willow, woven so fine,
They carry the fruits that will make sacred wine.

Saguaro's white flowers will bloom by starlight.
Reflecting the moon, they shine in the night.
The blooms become fruits, sweet, juicy and red.
Their juice brings rain magic, the elders have said.

Tall cactus with arms curving graceful and thin
Will reach out for water when cool rains begin.
With roots that are shallow and spread all around,
They will soak up the rain washing over hard ground.

The life-giving clouds, tremendous and white,
Build over far mountains, still out of sight.
Clouds swollen with rain that's waiting to fall
Will bring cooling water for one and for all.

Then catching the wind with the feathers he bound,
The medicine man makes circles around.
While the People hold hands and dance in a chain,
The singer's gourd rattle makes music like rain.

Grandfather's fire burns hot like the sun.
It cooks the ripe fruits till the syrup is done.
Grandmother's basket is woven just so
To capture the seeds and let syrup flow.

In morning's soft light, the women arrive
To pick the ripe fruits we will need to survive.
In baskets of willow, woven so fine,
They carry the fruits that will make sacred wine.

Saguaro's white flowers, like stars in the night,
Reflect the bright moon with a radiant light.
These blooms become fruits, sweet, juicy and red.
Their juice brings rain magic, the People have said.

Tall cactus with arms bending and thin
Will swell up with water when sweet rains begin.
With roots that are shallow and spread all around,
They will soak up the rain washing over hard ground.

The life-giving clouds, colossal and white,
Stop over far mountains, just out of sight.
Clouds swollen with rain that's waiting to fall
Will bring cooling water for one and for all.

And now comes the headman who blesses the wine
And elders who guard it until the right time.
Then all of the People are gathered together
To sing sacred songs to encourage the weather.

And catching the wind with the feathers he bound,
The medicine man makes circles around.
While the People hold hands and dance in a chain,
The singer's gourd rattle makes music like rain.

Grandfather's fire burns hot like the sun
And cooks the ripe fruits till the syrup is done.
Grandmother's basket is woven just so
To capture the seeds and let syrup flow.

In soft morning light, the women arrive
To harvest the fruits we will need to survive.
In baskets of willow, woven so fine,
They carry the fruits that will make sacred wine.

Saguaro's white flowers bloom by starlight.
Reflecting the moon, they enchant the warm night.
These blooms become fruits, sweet, juicy and red.
Their juice brings rain magic, the old stories said.

Tall cactus with arms reaching out long and thin
Will fatten with water when cloudbursts begin.
With roots that are shallow and spread all around,
They will soak up the rain washing over hard ground.

The life-giving clouds, gigantic in height,
Spill over the mountains and darken daylight.
Clouds swollen with rain that's waiting to fall
Will bring cooling water for one and for all.

Then out of the east comes a streak of bright light—
It flashes and dashes, then slithers from sight.
The deep ravines echo with thundering claps,
And even old dogs wake up from their naps.

The air fills with moisture—the earth smells alive.
Life springs from the rain—the desert will thrive.
The washes are flowing to soften hard ground—
Swift, rushing water—a mystical sound.

Thanks to the women, the headman, the wine,
To the fruits that are harvested each summertime.
The cactus, their flowers, sweet blessings abound.
They all work together to sing the rain down.

The life-giving clouds, enormous and white,
Flowed over the mountains, a beautiful sight!
The bountiful clouds let precious rain fall
To bring cooling water—for one and for all.

Choral Reading

Before 1970, the Tohono O'odham did not have a written language. Their cultural and spiritual beliefs and history were preserved and passed down through stories, songs, and orations. In the spirit of this rich tradition, *Sing Down the Rain* was written to be performed orally, with different voices taking the parts of the poem.

There are eight parts in the text: narrator, clouds, saguaros, flowers, women, grandparents, medicine man, and headman. The narrator begins the poem by reading the first four stanzas and ends the poem with: "Then out of the east . . ." The final two stanzas can be read by the narrator or by all the voices in unison. The cloud voice has the greatest number of repetitions; the headman has just one stanza.

To facilitate the choral reading, create a transcript of the poem with each voice highlighted. Each part can be read by one person or by a small group. The strong rhythm of the piece is designed to help readers move through the story together. A drum or rattle would be an appropriate instrument to provide a steady beat for the readers. The readers should also stand or be seated in the order of their stanzas.

Effective choral readings require that readers actively listen as well as speak. Practice is essential in choral readings, especially if more than one person is performing each voice.

The oral tradition continues to be a key aspect of modern-day Tohono O'odham culture. Please speak and perform this poem with the reverence and respect with which it was written.

Glossary

gourd a fruit that grows on a vine, similar to pumpkin and squash. Many gourds have hard rinds or shells that, when dried, can be made into utensils and musical instruments.

headman a Tohono O'odham elder who leads in a ceremony such as the wine ceremony.

mesquite a deep-rooted tree with bean-like seed pods. The beans are eaten by the O'odham, and the seed pods are used for horse and cattle feed. Mesquite wood is very hard and is used for cooking and as posts for ramadas and houses.

ravine a narrow valley created by running water.

saguaro a cactus that grows only in southeast Arizona, southeast California, and northwest Mexico. It can live more than 150 years and can grow more than fifty feet tall and weigh as much as ten tons. The saguaro has a column-like trunk that expands to hold and store rain. Its flower is the Arizona state flower.

wash a usually dry creek bed that carries water that runs off a mountain or high land during a heavy rain storm.

willow a tree or shrub with tough, slender, straight branches that was used in traditional O'odham baskets. Today the People make baskets from yucca and bear grass.

About the Author

JUDI MOREILLON is a professional storyteller and a school librarian in Tucson, Arizona. In addition to her teaching credential, Judi holds a Masters Degree in Library Science from the University of Arizona, where she regularly teaches courses in school librarianship. Judi also conducts storytelling workshops for children, librarians, and classroom teachers. In a previous school library position, Judi had the opportunity to work and learn with students from the Tohono O'odham Nation. The children generously shared their traditions and many stories with her. This poem, Judi's first book, is a gift to those children.

About the Illustrator

Tohono O'odham watercolor artist MICHAEL CHIAGO has painted the everyday and ceremonial life of his people for twenty-seven years. He has created murals, designed posters, and displayed his award-winning original paintings across the United States and abroad. He is a familiar figure at the Heard Museum in Phoenix, where he has participated in shows and demonstrated his art. In 1996, he accompanied the Heard's traveling exhibition, "Rain," to the British Museum of Man in London, where he was artist in residence. He states, " I'm proud of my Tohono O'odham heritage, and I work hard to keep it strong. I hope that young readers will share the joy I have felt while painting the illustrations for *Sing Down the Rain*."